Julian Marshall

Handbook of Engravers of Ornament

SALZWASSER VERLAG

Julian Marshall

Handbook of Engravers of Ornament

1st Edition | ISBN: 978-3-84605-882-4

Place of Publication: Frankfurt am Main, Germany

Year of Publication: 2020

Salzwasser Verlag GmbH, Germany.

Reprint of the original, first published in 1869.

HANDBOOK

OF ·

ENGRAVERS OF ORNAMENT.

PRODUCED FOR THE

USE OF SCHOOLS OF ART; AND, GENERALLY, FOR PUBLIC
INSTRUCTION.

By JULIAN MARSHALL.

LONDON:
PRINTED BY GEORGE E. EYRE AND WILLIAM SPOTTISWOODE,
PRINTERS TO THE QUEEN'S MOST EXCELLENT MAJESTY.
FOR HER MAJESTY'S STATIONERY OFFICE.
1869.

Price Sixpence.

mental subjects, invented and engraved by men who are obscure and nearly forgotten, which in most cases show evidence of very great talent, study, and industry. On the other hand, again, in the engraved works of A. Dürer, M. Schongauer, A. Mantegna, Lucas van Leyden, and others of similar rank in the aristocracy of Art, the student will find, not only a vast mass of useful details of armour, costume, furniture, jewels, architecture, and the like, but also many plates devoted to the delineation or designing of *objects-of-Art*, of various kinds. These, coming from such a source, are of the greatest importance and value.

Examples of many of these works are found, appropriately placed, in the South Kensington Museum, where they should be of the greatest use to the student. The collection already includes specimens of very many of the artists who are named in our list ; and it will be wise to increase their number and variety as often as opportunities may occur. Although, in point of brilliance of impression or purity of preservation, many of these specimens leave something to be desired ; yet they suffice to show us the design and intention of the artist, which though imperfectly seen, are still exceedingly valuable.*

It is not necessary to say more, in this place, than to commend the works of these decorative designers of all ages to the modern student of that branch of Art ; in them he will find an almost inexhaustible mine of wealth, ready to his eye and hand. Without slavishly copying the designs of those great masters, he may learn from them the proper manner of treating such subjects as he may choose, and acquire the secret of making ornament beautiful, but subservient to its purpose.

In order to set clearly forth the history of the origin and growth of the art, a tabular and chronological arrangement of the artists' names, in their different schools, has been appended, in the form of an index.

Julian Marshall.

---

* References will be found in the body of the work to the collections in the Print Room of the British Museum as well as to the National Art Library at South Kensington, for the works of engravers that are likely to be of especial service to the student. In many instances no reference could be made to the latter collection. It is very desirable that such deficiencies in the contents of the South Kensington Art Library should be made up as soon as circumstances will permit.

A CHRONOLOGICAL TABLE

OF

THE ENGRAVERS OF ORNAMENT

OF

THE SCHOOLS OF

ITALY.	GERMANY.	HOLLAND and NETHERLANDS.	FRANCE.	ENGLAND.
Finiguerra, M. b. 1415.				
	Mecheln, J. f. 1460–80.			
Mantegna, A. b. 1431.—d. 1506.	Walch, J. f. 1480.			
Peregrini da Cesena. f. 1500.	Schön, M. b. 1450.—d. 1499.			
Modena, N. da b. 1460.			Jollat. f. 1510.	
Zoan Andrea. f. 1515.	Goar, Van. f. 1516.			
	Dürer, A. b. 1471.—d. 1528.			
	Wilborn, N. f. 1530–36.			
	Burgkmair, H. b. 1472.—d. 1559.			
Raimondi, M. A. b. 1487.—d. 1540.	Altdorfer, A. b. 1488.—d. 1538.			
	Apsch, J. A. b. 1490.—d. 1556.			
Veneziano, A. b. 1490.	Bink, J. b. 1490 or 1504.			
Ravenna, M. b. 1496.	Beham, B. b. 1490.—d. 1540.	Leyden, L. b. 1494.—d. 1533.		
	Beham, H. S. b. 1500.—d. 1550.			
	Weigel, H. f. 1535.—d. 1590.			
	Pencz, G. b. 1500.—d. 1550.			
	Aldegrever, H. b. 1502.			
	Treu, M. f. 1540.			
	Kerver, J. f. 1540.			

b. born.　　d. died.　　f. flourished.

A Chronological Table of the Engravers of Ornament of the Schools of

Italy.	Germany.	Holland and Netherlands.	France.	England.
——	Heuman, G. D. f. 1724.	——	——	——
——	Pfeffel, J. A. b. 1674.—d. 1750.	——	——	——
——	Rademacker, A. b. 1675.—d. 1735.	——	——	——
——	——	——	Meissonier, J. A. b. 1695.	——
——	——	——	Papillon, J. B. M. b. 1698.—d. 1776.	——
——	——	——	Fourdrinière, P. f. 1730.	——
——	——	——	Blondel, J. F. f. 1740.	Toms, W. H. f. 1740.
——	——	——	Quillart, P. A. b. 1711.	Bowles, T. b. 1712.
Nolli, G. B. f. 1755.	——	——	Moreau, P. f. 1750.	Rooker, E. b. 1712.
——	——	——	——	Langley, J. B. d. 1751.
Orazzi, N. f. 1760.	——	——	Vauquer, J. f. 1760.	——
——	——	——	Bouchard, J. f. 1760.	——
——	——	——	Cochin, C. N. (the younger). b. 1715.—d. 1788.	——
——	——	——	Saly, J. F. b. 1717.—d. 1776.	——
Piranesi, G. B. b. 1721.—d. 1779.	——	——	Patte, P. b. 1723.—d. 1780.	Parr, R. b. 1723.
Piranesi, F.	——	——	Galimard, C. b. 1729.	——
Morghen, P. b. 1730.	——	——	Taraval, L. G. b. 1737.	——
Bartolozzi, F. b. 1730.—d. 1813.	——	——	Nicolet, B. A. b. 1740.—d. 1807.	Basire, J. b. 1740.
——	——	——	Vinsac, C. D. b. 1749.	——
Piranesi, L. b. 1750.	Schlicht, A. b. 1754.—d. 1826.	——	Poulleau. b. 1749.	——
——	Rupprecht, F. C. b. 1779.—d. 1831.	——	Guerin, C. b. 1758.	Lowry, W. b. 1770.—d. 1824.
——	——	——	——	Neale, J. P. b. 1770.—d. 1848.
——	——	——	——	Le Keux, J. b. 1783.—d. 1846.
——	——	——	Jacquemart, J. F. b. 1837.	——

HANDBOOK OF ENGRAVERS OF ORNAMENT.

ALBERTI, Cherubino, born at Borgo S. Sepolcro 1552; died 1615. Instructed in the art by his father, Michele Alberti, and became a reputable painter of historical subjects. He is, however, more celebrated as an engraver. His plates are executed entirely with the graver, and it does not appear that he made use of the etching-needle. Some of the beautiful friezes by Polidoro da Cara- 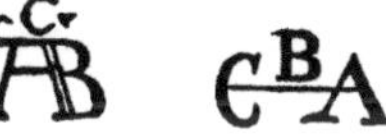 vaggio, painted on the façades of public edifices, which have been destroyed by time, are preserved to us in the works of this master. He also engraved a piece of architecture, after Il Rosso, in two prints. Roma, 1475. His works are very numerous.

Prints by this artist in the Collection at South Kensington. (The numbers refer to Bartsch's Catalogue.)

B. 6. Judith with the head of Holofernes.

B. 130. A winged figure holding in one hand a globe with the arms of the Medici, and a trumpet and palm branch in the other. Inscribed VNITA VIRTVS.

B. 145. A winged figure standing on a globe marked with the arms of the Barberini. No. 1.

B. 150. A nude figure of a man, seated and turned to the left; after Michael Angelo.

Two plates of Amorini, after designs by Alberti, mentioned by Bartsch, v. 17, p. 119.

Also an original drawing of festoons supported by two Amorini.

A few examples of this artist are in the British Museum.

ALDEGREVER, Heinrich, born at Zoust, in Westphalia, 1502; date of death uncertain.* He went to Nuremberg for the purpose of becoming a pupil of Durer, whose manner he followed, both as a painter and as an engraver, and became one of the most distin- guished of the so-called " Little Masters." His execution is very neat and finished, and he worked entirely with the graver. His design, without being incorrect, must however be allowed to be Gothic, though not more so than that of other artists of his time. He usually marked his plates with the cipher His works are very numerous. Latest dated work, 1555. Among his works we find about 100 vignettes, ornamental  designs of scroll-work, grotesques, arabes- ques, chased dagger-sheaths, &c. All of these are interesting, and

---

many are of the greatest beauty; they may be of great use to
the designers of ornamental work in the various metals and other
materials.

There is a very fine and almost complete collection of his works in the
British Museum. The South Kensington Museum also possesses about 50
prints by this artist, and the collection might with advantage be increased.

ALTDORFER, Albrecht, born at Altdorff, in Bavaria, 1488;
died 1538. A painter and a more eminent engraver, said to have
been a pupil of Albert Durer. He holds a
very respectable rank among those artists
who are called the "Little Masters;" and
his wooden cuts, which are by far the best
of his performances, nearly approach the
excellence of those of Holbein. His entire work, on wood and
copper, is upwards of 170 prints. After filling various important
posts in Ratisbon, he was appointed architect to the town.

There are several of the prints of goblets and other works by this artist
preserved at South Kensington.

A very fine collection of his works is in the British Museum, including an
almost complete set of the goblets and vases, which are extremely rare.

AMMAN, Justus, born at Zurich 1539; died at Nuremberg
1591. A painter and an engraver, chiefly excellent in the last-
named art. His works in stained glass
were richly and brilliantly coloured. His
pen drawings partake of the spirit and
neatness of his prints. The number of his
works amounts to upwards of 550 prints.
He is ranked among the "Little Masters." He engraved on both
wood and copper. His drawing is in general tolerably correct,
his execution smart and spirited, and his manner of engraving is
neat and decided.

In the South Kensington Library are found books illustrated by Amman
(see Universal Catalogue of Books on Art). Very nearly all the works of
Amman are found in the collections at the British Museum.

ANDREANI, Andrea, born at Mantua 1560; died 1623;
a painter and very celebrated engraver. He worked
chiefly as an engraver from an early period of his life
in Rome, some time after the art of engraving on wood
had been first practised by Hugo da Carpi. His
works are confined to wooden cuts, which are printed
in chiaroscuro, that is, from different blocks for the different co-
lours. His drawing is correct, his execution neat and spirited,
and his style masterly. The number of prints attributed to him
is very considerable. Among the most interesting is the Triumph
of Julius Cæsar, in ten sheets, with the title; *after And.
Mantegna*, MDXCVIII.

An example of this series is at South Kensington, as well as a chiaroscuro
print, after G. da Bologna, representing the condemnation of Christ by Pilate.

A fine collection of Andreani's works is preserved in the British Museum.

APSCH, Hieronymus Andreas, born at Nuremberg, circa
1490; died 1556. He assisted Hans Burgkmair in executing the

wood cuts for a book published at Vienna, entitled "Der Weyss König," containing the principal events of the life and reign of the Emperor Maximilian I. They consisted of 237 prints.

A copy of the above-mentioned book is in the Art Library, South Kensington.

AQUILA, Francesco Faraone, born at Palermo 1676; date of death not known. He was the elder brother of the celebrated Pietro Aquila, and established himself at Rome about 1700. His engravings are numerous, and some of them highly esteemed; and among them a circular print, the First Vault in the Vatican, *after Ciro Ferri*, 1696. Two cupolas, *after P. da Cortona;* circular. Another cupola, *after the same*, circular; and three large prints of the vault of St. Francis Xavier at Naples, *after Paolo de Mattei.*

In the Art Library, South Kensington, is an ob. fol. book, entitled "Picturæ Raphaelis Sanctij Urbinatis ex Aulâ et conclavibus Palatij Vaticani," 1722; the plates are engraved by F. Aquila.

AQUILA, Pietro, was the younger brother of F. Aquila, and was with him at Rome, about the year 1700. He was a respectable painter, but much more famous as an engraver. His drawing is extremly correct, and he etched his plates in a bold and free manner. The number of his works is very considerable, and among them we may notice the Farnese Gallery, in 25 plates, with the statues and ornaments, and the chamber of the Farnese Palace, in 13 plates, inscribed *Imagines Farnesiani Cubiculi.*

In the Art Library, South Kensington, is a volume of engravings by Pietro Aquila, entitled "Galeriæ Farnesianæ Icones," ob. fol. n. d. (? 1693).

AUDENAERDE, Robert van, born at Ghent 1663; date of death not known; a reputable painter, and a still more celebrated engraver. He was first a scholar of Francis van Mierhop, but afterwards studied under John van Cleef. When he was twenty-two years of age he went to Rome, where he became a pupil of Carlo Maratti, who recommended him to devote himself entirely to the art of engraving.

In the collection, South Kensington, is a set of 10 plates (with the title) engraved by him after A. Mantegna's Triumphs of Julius Cæsar. fol. Some examples of this artist are also in the collection at the British Museum.

AUDRAN, Gérard, born at Lyons 1640; died at Paris 1703. The son of Claude Audran, and the nephew of Charles. Studied under his father, and afterwards under his uncle in Paris, where he remained some time. He then visited Rome, and there studied under Carlo Maratti. Having made himself a considerable reputation, he was invited to return to Paris by Colbert, and was appointed engraver to the King. He became connected with Le Brun, after whose pictures he engraved his principal plates, the Battles of Alexander. His works are very numerous. Among the most interesting to the student of ornamental art are 46 ceilings and monumental paintings, 19 vignettes for books, &c., 24 emblematical designs, 17 subjects of statuary, and 30 plates

illustrating a book by the artist, entitled "LES PROPORTIONS DU
"CORPS HUMAIN, *mesurées sur les plus belles figures de l'anti-*
"*quité. Paris. Girard Audran, 1683.*" fol.

Some of this artist's works are in the collection at the British Museum, and
a few examples in the South Kensington collection.

BARRIÈRE, Dominique, born at Marseilles, circa 1622 ; date
of death not known; an ingenious French engraver. His principal
residence was at Rome, where he engraved a considerable number
of plates, in a neat manner like that of Stefano della Bella. He
sometimes signed his plates with his name *Dominicus Barriere
Massiliensis,* and sometimes with the cipher. Among
others we have the following prints by him :—Seven
views of the Villa Aldobrandini, 1649. *Pontana
maggiore nel Giardino di Tivoli :*—Eighty-four views
and statues of the Villa Pamphili. Four, entitled
Catafalco e apparato nella chiesa, &c. Sepulchral monument
of N. L. Plumbini. Hercules, after a basso-relievo in the garden
of the Medici.

He is fairly represented in the British Museum. No specimens worthy of
mention at South Kensington.

BARTOLI, Pietro Santo, born at Perugia, circa 1635; date
of death not known; sometimes called Il Perugino. In the early
part of his life he practised painting, but abandoned it to devote
himself entirely to engraving, in which he greatly distinguished
himself. His plates are chiefly etched, and his point is extremely
free and masterly. Their number is very considerable; among
them we may notice :—VARIOUS ANTIQUITIES. *Admiranda
Romanorum Antiquitatum ac veteris Sculpturæ Vestigia,* 83
plates. *Romanæ magnitudinis Monumenta,* 138 plates. *Veteres
arcus Augustorum triumphis insignes,* 52 plates. *Colonna di
Marco Aurelio,* &c., the Antonine column, 78 plates. *Colonna
Trajana, di Alfonso Ciacconi,* 128 plates. *Sepolcri autichi
Romani ed Etruschi trovati in Roma,* 123 plates. The Aqueduct
that brings the water from Civita Vecchia, four large plates. The
Sepulchral Urn, in the court of the Capitol. *Le antiche lucerne
sepolcrali in Roma,* 1691 and 1704, 119 plates. Theatre erected in
St. Peter's for the canonization of two saints, from his own
design. The Sepulchral Monument of Pope Urban VIII., from
his own design. An ancient Mausoleum, after a design by *P. da
Cortona.* (See Nagler, *Künstler Lexicon.*)

A complete collection of his works is in the Library, British Museum. A
good number of his books in the Library, South Kensington.

BARTOLOZZI, Francesco, born at Florence 1730 ; died at
Lisbon 1813. He was instructed in drawing by Hugfort Ferretti
at Florence, and learnt the art of engraving from Joseph Wagner
at Venice. His first plates were engraved while in the employment of Wagner. In 1764 he came to England. He has left us
a prodigious number of plates, many of which are of an ornamental character, and entitle him justly to a high place among
engravers of that class of subject. Among a multitude of plates,
we may notice the following, as peculiarly interesting under

that head :—A collection of gems, designed by various artists, and engraved by *Bartolozzi*. A large number of book-plates, tickets, and other ornamental designs.

A very fine collection, amounting to perhaps more than a thousand examples, is in the Print Room, British Museum. Some specimens of minor importance at South Kensington. He might be more fully represented.

BASIRE, James, born at London 1740 ; little is known of the circumstances of his life. He engraved some of the plates which illustrate the publications of the Society of Antiquaries.

Some fine examples of his work are in the Print Room, British Museum.

BAUDOUIN, Antoine François, born at Dixmunde, in Flanders, 1640 ; died at Paris, 1700. He first studied painting under F. A. van der Meulen, but afterwards devoted himself entirely to engraving. His plates are chiefly after the pictures or designs of Vandermeulen, and are etched in a free, bold style, producing a good effect. Among his works we may notice the following architectural and ornamental engravings :—Six views of towns in France. Two views of Versailles; as it was, and as it is. View of the castle of Vincennes. View of the Palace of Fontainebleau, two sheets. Two views of gardens in Italy, after A. Genoels.

BEATRIZET, or BEAUTRIZET, Nicolas, born at Lunéville, in Lorraine, circa 1515; died circa 1560. The greater part of his life was passed in Italy, and most of his works are from works or monuments preserved at Rome. His plates generally resemble in manner of execution those of the school of Raimondi. Among his numerous prints we may here notice the following :—Forty-three plates, illustrating the anatomy of the human body, by Jean Valverde. Eleven statues and bas-reliefs, from the antique. Twelve architectural subjects and plans of towns. An ample catalogue of the works of this artist will be found in the Peintre-Graveur Français of M. Robert Dumesnil, tom. ix.

A nearly complete collection of his works is in the Print Room, British Museum. No worthy examples of him at South Kensington.

BEHAM, Bartel, born at Nuremberg, circa 1490 ; died 1540. He was twice in Italy, where he spent many years of his life, and where he died. He studied under Raimondi, both at Rome and Bologna. His design is masterly and correct, and his execution, while admirably delicate, is also free and harmonious. Bartsch gives us a good catalogue of his works, among which the most interesting to the student of ornamental art are the following :—B. 44. A triumphal procession; a conqueror in a chariot, preceded and followed by several female figures carrying vases, torches, palm branches, &c. B. 51. Nude child with scroll work of foliage; a very fine plate. B. 52. A genius holding a shield ; a very pretty piece. B. 53. The coat of arms with the cock.

B. 54. Panel of ornament, with three children supporting a vase. Five other ornamental and heraldic designs and vignettes.

In the British Museum is preserved a nearly complete collection of the works of Bartel Beham. A few specimens of his work are in the South Kensington collection.

BEHAM, Hans Sebald, born at Nuremberg 1500; died at Frankfort 1550; the nephew, and at first the pupil, of Bartel Beham. He afterwards received instruction from Albert Durer. He lived in his native town till the year 1540, and established himself subsequently at Frankfort. He is very celebrated as an engraver. His prints approach those of his uncle very nearly in excellence. He also designed a quantity of subjects upon wooden blocks. We have about 260 prints by him, and 171 wooden cuts from his designs. Among the engravings we may notice briefly the following, as most interesting from our present point of view:—B. 221, 222. Two plates, representing three medals and their reverses. B. 223–237. Fourteen vignettes of various kinds. B. 238–259. Twenty-one vases, ornamental panels, capitals of columns, &c.

A nearly complete collection of these prints is in the Print Room, British Museum. He is fairly represented at South Kensington.

BELLA, Stefano della, born at Florence 1610; died at Florence 1664. The son of a goldsmith, and said to have been intended for his father's trade; but was placed under Cesare Dandini, to learn painting. A decided inclination for the art of engraving induced his father to permit him to become a pupil of Canta Gallina, who was also the master of Callot. No artist has handled the point with more facility and finesse; his execution is admirable, and his touch spirited and picturesque. He designed his plates with infinite taste, and they produce a clear and brilliant effect. His works in number exceed 1,400. Among his principal prints we may notice:—A basso-relievo, antique; after Polidoro. Another, antique; a woman stopping a bull. Perspective view of the Catafalco of the Emperor Ferdinand II., with the arms of the Medici. A thesis, on the canonization of Francis Solanus, 1639. Plan of the siege of La Rochelle. Plan of the siege of Arras. The Reposoir, or Fête Dieu; lengthwise. The view of the Pont Neuf, Paris. View of the castle of S. Angelo. Six prints of vases. Four views of Roman ruins. Twenty-four views of edifices; published by Israel Silvestre. Eighteen, called *Raccolta di vari capricci.*

A fine collection, probably complete, of his works is in the Print Room, British Museum. At South Kensington there is a considerable number of his ornaments and a few figures.

BERNARD, Salomon, or Little Bernard, born at Lyons 1512; date of death not known. He executed a number of wood cuts for the booksellers, which are well designed, and cut with great spirit and neatness. His best prints are those which he made for the Bible which was published at Lyons, at different times, from 1550 to 1580. Besides these, we have by him the following :—A set of medals for the Epitome of the Antiquities of Giacomo Strada, of Mantua; published at Lyons in 1553. Eighteen of baths; printed at Lyons in 1572. A set of vignettes for the French translation of Virgil; Lyons, 1560. Twenty-two of theatrical decorations. According to Brulliot he was living in 1598.

A complete collection of his works is in the Library, British Museum. No specimens worthy of mention at South Kensington.

BINK, Jacob, born at Nuremberg or Cologne, 1490 or 1504. He signs himself Coloniensis on one of his prints. His works, being signed with different ciphers, have given rise to many discussions, a full account of which, and of the works themselves, will be found in Bartsch, v. 8. His style resembles that of Aldegrever, but has more facility. He is ranked among the "Little Masters." His drawing is correct, and marked with more taste than that of others of his contemporaries. The works of Bink amount to nearly 100. Among them we may notice nine vignettes, panels of ornament, and a design for a sheath; all of which are distinguished by a good style and great delicacy of treatment.

A nearly complete collection of his works is in the Print Room, British Museum. Several specimens at South Kensington.

BISCHOP, Jan de, born at the Hague, 1646; died at Amsterdam, 1686. A designer and engraver, originally intended for the law, according to Houbraken. His favourite amusement was drawing; but as an engraver he is still more deserving of notice, and he has left a large number of plates, principally etched, and harmonized with the graver in a free and pleasing manner. There is great relief and richness in his prints. His most important work was a set of prints for a book, entitled *Paradigmata graphices variorum artiphicum, tabulis æneis. Pars I. et II. Hagæ*, 1671, *fol.* The first edition, published by the author, contains 102 plates. The second, published by Nic. Vischer, the same year, contains 113 plates. This engraver latinized his name and assumed that of Episcopus (for Bischop), on which account he marked his plates with a cipher, composed of the letters J. E., thus—

A complete set of his prints is in the Print Room, British Museum.

BLOND, Michel le, born 1580; date of death not known. A native of Frankfort, who resided chiefly at Amsterdam, and appears to have been employed principally in designing ornaments for the goldsmiths. In 1626 he published a set of ornaments, foliage, fruit, and flowers, engraved with great neatness. His prints, which are all very small, are executed entirely with the graver in the finished manner of Theodore de Bry. He sometimes marked his plates with a cipher composed of an M and a B, thus, **M̲B̲** We have the following plates by him :—St. Jerome seated at a desk writing, with an ornamental border; a small circular plate, about the size of a shilling, dated 1610. Figures dancing, in a small oval, with an ornamental border, signed *M. Blondus*, 1612. The representation of a marriage, *M. Blondus*, 1615. Two ornaments for goldsmiths, inscribed *Wilhelm van Weelichkeit*. A very small plate of ornaments with three goblets. Six plates numbered, of arabesque ornaments for knife-handles, *Michael Blondus fecit;* very highly finished.

A fine collection of his works is in the Print Room, British Museum. A good many of his ornaments are in the South Kensington collection.

BLONDEL, Jean François, flourished circa 1740 at Paris; published a description of the festivities given by the City of Paris in 1740, on the marriage of Mme. Louise Elisabeth of France with Don Philip, Infant of Spain. The plates, representing the temporary buildings, fireworks, &c., are chiefly engraved by himself. He also etched the plates for some large volumes of Architecture, published by himself.

A good many of his ornaments are in the South Kensington collection.

BOISSIÈRE, Simon de la, circa 1680. A French engineer, also distinguished as an engraver, having executed several plates after his own designs as well as from those of others. We have by him 41 plates of antique medals, in the Royal French collection. A view of the Palais Royal, in two sheets. Several plates for the work called *Traité des Edifices Antiques de Rome,* by A. Desgodets, published at Paris in 1682.

A complete and very fine collection of his works is in the Print Room, British Museum, and examples in the South Kensington collection.

BOS. *See* BUS.

BOUCHARD, Joseph, circa 1760. A French engraver, to whom we owe several plates of buildings and antiquities, executed in a neat and finished style.

BOULANGER, Jean, born at Troyes, 1613; date of death not known. A French engraver, who at first imitated the polished manner of Fr. Poilly, but afterwards adopted the dotted style of Morin. His plates have considerable merit. Among others he engraved The pompous Cavalcade on the occasion of Louis XIV. coming of age.

BOWLES, Thomas, born in London, circa 1712; date of death not known. This artist published a set of 30 views of the public edifices in and near London, of which some of the plates were engraved by himself; among them are,—A view of London from the Thames, 1751. Somerset House, 1753. Greenwich Hospital, 1745. The Royal Exchange, and others.

A few specimens of his work are in the Print Room, British Museum.

BRUYN, Abraham de, born at Antwerp, circa 1540. He is ranked among the little masters. His plates are entirely the work of the graver, in a neat, formal style; and his drawing is not always correct. Among his principal works we may notice,—A set of plates entitled *Imperii ac Sacerdotii ornatus, &c.*, 1577. A set of plates, *Diversarum gentium armatura equestris*, 1577. A set of small friezes of Hunting and Hawking, 1565. A set of arabesque patterns.

He is fairly represented in the Print Room, British Museum. A few examples by him are in the South Kensington collection.

BRY, or BRIE, Theodor de, born at Liege, 1528 ; died at Frankfort, 1598. An eminent German engraver, who resided chiefly at Frankfort, where he carried on the business of selling books and prints. He seems to have formed his style on that of H. S. Beham, and he worked almost entirely with the graver, in a neat but free manner, well adapted to the subjects he chose, such as public processions and parades, in which he drew the numerous figures correctly, giving much expression to the heads. He engraved the plates for the first four volumes of Boissard's Antiquities ; the remaining two were finished by his sons. We have also by him the following : Several designs for saucers, with portraits, masks, and grotesques ; circular. Two medallions of Scanderbegus, and his wife, in borders of flowers, insects, and birds, with Latin inscription. The procession of the funeral of Sir Philip Sidney, in 34 plates. The procession of the Knights of the Garter in 1576, dated 1578, in 12 plates. The plates for the work published at Frankfort, 1596, *Hariot's brief, true report of Virginia*. (Picart copied these plates for his *Religious Ceremonies of all nations*.) The plates for the Latin narrative of the cruelties of the Spaniards in America, 1598, 123 plates. The plates for his great work, *Descriptio generalis totius Indiæ, Orientalis et Occidentalis*, in 19 parts, in five vols., folio. 1598.

He is fairly represented in the Print Room, British Museum. There are a good many specimens of his work at South Kensington.

BRY, or BRIE, Johann Theodor de, born at Liege 1561. The elder son of the preceding artist. He much assisted his father in the great works which he executed ; and with his brother J. Israel, completed the two last volumes of *Boissard's Roman Antiquities*, left unfinished at his father's death. We have also by him many other works, including some friezes after Titian, of soldiers marching, &c.

He is fairly represented in the Print Room, British Museum.

23959.

BURGKMAIR, Hans, born at Augsburg 1472; died 1559. A contemporary and friend of Dürer, and founder of a school of his own. In his native city are preserved many of his pictures. His prints are entirely engraved on wood and executed with great spirit; they are very numerous. Among them we may mention, The portrait of the Emperor Maximilian, 1508, chiaro-scuro. A set of 137 plates for a book, published at Vienna, *Der Weyss König;* giving the principal actions of Maximilian. A set of 38 plates of the triumphal entry of Maximilian I.

A very fine, if not complete, series of his works is in the Print Room, British Museum. At South Kensington is a set of the Triumph of Maximilian.

BUS, BOS, or VANDEN BOSCH, Cornelius, born at Bois le Duc, 1510. It appears that he studied in Italy, as his style resembles that of M. da Ravenna, though it is inferior. His plates are executed with the graver entirely. Among his best works are found,—A set of 16 of trophies, arms, and grotesques, Rome 1550 to 1553. The equestrian statue of Marcus Aurelius, and many others.

He is fairly represented in the Print Room, British Museum. A few of his ornaments are in the South Kensington collection.

CALLOT, Jacques, born at Nancy 1593; died at Nancy 1635. An ingenious designer and admirable engraver, the son of a gentleman of noble family, and originally intended by his parents for a very different profession. He, however, left home with a company of Bohemians, went to Florence, devoted himself to the arts, and studied under Canta Gallina. He afterwards was allowed by his parents to go to Rome; and in 1628 he went to Paris, when he became famous by his views of the sieges of Rochelle and the Isle de Ré. His plates amount to about 1,500 in number, are remarkable for spirit, delicacy, and expression; and some of them contain great numbers of figures. Among the most interesting to us, are,—A view of the Louvre. A companion view, of the Pont Neuf. The Parterre of Nancy, and other similar plates. The Siege of the Isle de Ré, in 16 sheets. The Siege of Rochelle; similar. The Siege of Breda. Fourteen plates of Military Exercises. Fourteen of Fantasies, 1635. Twelve of Ladies and Gentlemen, in the dresses of the mode. Three of Festivals during the Carnival at Florence. Seven of Tournaments. Four of Jousts and Tiltings. For a list of his works see U. Cat. of Books on Art, Callot (J.).

There is a very fine collection of his works in the British Museum. Some few specimens of this ingenious artist are in the South Kensington collection; some are late impressions; and he might be more largely represented with advantage.

CARAGLIO, Giovanni Giacomo, born at Verona, circa 1512; died circa 1570. Generally considered to have been a pupil of Marc Antonio Raimondi. His drawing is correct, and he holds a high place among the engravers of Italy. He was much employed in the graving of gems, and executed several medals, by which he gained great reputation at the court of Sigismund, King of Poland.

A fine collection of his prints is in the British Museum.

CASTIGLIONE, Giovanni Benedetto, born at Genoa 1616; died 1670. An eminent painter, and also remarkable for having executed a number of plates, partly with the etching needle, and partly with the burin, in a most masterly style. Among them we may mention,   —A Man with some pieces of armour, and another examining a tomb. A Bacchanal with a Satyr on a pedestal. Eleven plates of vignettes, &c.

A fine collection of his works is in the British Museum.

CHAVEAU, François, born at Paris 1613; died at Paris 1676. A painter, but more distinguished as an engraver. He executed a great number of plates for the booksellers, in which we find force, fire, and ingenuity. His smaller plates are much in the manner of S. le Clerc, and are his best pieces. His works amount to nearly 3,000 plates, most of them illustrating various books. He also executed 243 plates of medals, the collection of *F. Orsini.* The Triumphal Arch for the Place Dauphine, *after Le Brun.*

At South Kensington is a set of masks by this artist. A few examples are also in the British Museum.

CLERC, Sebastien le, born at Mentz (Lorraine) 1637; died 1714. This admirable designer and engraver was the son of a goldsmith, who first taught him the principles of design, with the view of obtaining for him a situation in the corps of engineers. By the advice of Le Brun, however, he devoted himself entirely to the art of engraving. His style is excellent, being advanced principally with the etching point, and merely finished and coloured with the graver. Among his numerous plates, which amount to nearly 3,000, are found,—The Triumphal Arch for Louis XIV., at the Porte St. Antoine. The Elevation of the large Stones employed in building the front of the Louvre, 1677. The Chapel of S. Catherine at Stockholm, where is the sepulchre of the kings of Sweden, 1654. The monument of the King of Sweden. The Monument of the Chancellor Seguier. Thirty-two plates for Du Fresnoy's Art of Painting, Paris, 1673. Thirty-nine with the title, for *Le Labyrinthe de Versailles*, Paris, 1677. The Principles of Design, in 52 prints, by *S. le Clerc*, and many others of the same kind.

He is fairly represented in the British Museum. In the South Kensington collection is a set of the Conquests, and another of the illustrations to Æsop's Fables, by this artist.

CLEYN, or KLEYN, Francis de, born at Rostock (date uncertain); died 1658. A painter, in the employ of Christian IV. of Denmark for some time. He afterwards went to Rome for improvement, where he passed four years, and acquired a talent for designing grotesques, by which he afterwards distinguished himself. He came to England in the reign of James I., who employed him in designing grotesques for the manufacture of tapestry at Mortlake. He etched some plates in the manner of Hollar, among which are,—A set of five plates of the Senses, with grotesque ornaments. The Seven Liberal Arts ; *F. Cleyn, fecit,* 1645. A book of 10 plates of grotesque ornaments.

There is nothing of note by this artist at South Kensington. He is fairly represented in the British Museum collection.

COCHIN, Charles Nicolas, the younger, born at Paris 1715; died 1788 or 1790. Received his first instruction from his father, and became a very eminent designer and engraver. He executed an immense number of plates, many of which are frontispieces, vignettes, and other ornamental works ; all engraved with such taste and judgment that, if he had done nothing more important, they would have established his reputation. He engraved the Ceremony of the Marriage of the Dauphin 1745, and the Decoration of the Theatre of Versailles on that occasion, The Funeral Pomp of the Dauphiness at S. Denis, 1746, and several other funeral ceremonies.

At South Kensington are a few book illustrations by this artist ; and a few examples are also found in the British Museum.

COLLAERT, Hans, born at Antwerp, circa 1540, worked as late as 1622. After studying under his father, he went to Italy, where he passed some time. He engraved a great number of plates, with more taste and less stiffness than his father. Among them we find a set of 10, entitled *Monilium Bullarum in auriumque,* &c., 1581. He also executed titles to various works.

Some good specimens of designs for jewellery by this artist are in the South Kensington collection.
A good collection of his works is in the British Museum.

CORIOLANO, Giovanni Battista, born at Bologna, circa 1590 ; died 1649. He was both painter and engraver, but not much distinguished in the former art. He engraved both on wood and copper, but his wooden cuts are by far his best works. He executed the Triumphal Arch in honour of Louis XIII., *Il Coriolano, fec.,* and 27 plates of emblematical subjects : *after Paolo Macci.* (The whole set, *Paolo Macii Emblemata,* consists of 83 plates ; the rest are by *O. Gatti* and *A. Parasini.*) He also engraved a number of theses and frontispieces.

No specimens worthy of mention by this artist at South Kensington, but a fine collection of his works is in the British Museum.

DELAUNE, Etienne, born at Paris 1519 ; died at Paris 1583. This eminent artist was distinguished as a designer, goldsmith, engraver, and medallist. His manner is extremely bold and free, considering the very small size of most of his works and their very high finish of execution. In some of them he has introduced the manner called "*pointillé,*" or "*opus mallei,*" invented by early Italian artists, and practised especially by Giulio

Campagnola, but never by any French engraver before Delaune. His plates amount in number to about 450. Of these a large proportion are ornamental or decorative, 138 of them being designed specially for that purpose; comprising mirrors, whistles, handles for vases, bottoms of cups, door knockers, and various grotesques. Delaune is, perhaps, the most eminent of the class of engravers to which he belongs.

In the British Museum is a considerable collection of his works. He is also represented by some examples at South Kensington.

DELSENBACH, Johann Adam, flourished at Vienna about 1721. He engraved part of the plates for the History of Architecture, with views of the most famous buildings in the world, after the designs of *J. H. Fischers*, published at Vienna in 1721. Part of the views of the principal buildings in the city and suburbs of Vienna are by this artist.

DOLIVAR, Jean, born at Saragossa in 1641. He studied at Paris, and engraved some of the plates of ornamental and decorative subjects for *Berain's Ornaments*. He was also employed in the set of the little conquests of Louis XIV. His works are compared with those of Le Pautre and Chaveau, though they are not equal to either.

DU PERAC. *See* PERAC.

DÜRER, Albrecht, born at Nuremberg 1471; died at Nuremberg 1528. This distinguished artist, if not the founder of the German school, was at least one of the first that attempted to reform the barbarous taste and style of his country. He was the son of a goldsmith, who taught him the first elements of design, and who intended to bring him up to his own trade; the strong predilection, however, of the son for the liberal arts prevailed, and he was to have been sent to receive the instruction of Martin Schongauer at Colmar, but eventually was placed under Michael Wohlgemuth, from whom he received the principles of painting and engraving. He at the same time cultivated with great assiduity the study of perspective, mathematics, and architecture, in all of which he excelled. As an engraver he carried the art to a pitch of perfection in its infancy which has since been hardly surpassed. His design is stiff and formal like that of his contemporaries; but, at the same time, full of beauty, precision, and finished delicacy. Although he is not

an engraver of ornaments, his works are most interesting to students of that branch of art, for the ornamental detail, costume, and accessories, which are remarkable in many of his plates. It would be too tedious to mention all of these, but we may point out the following as among the most interesting in that respect :—The Melancholy, dated 1514. The Knight and Death, 1513. A Coat of Arms, with a young woman and Death. A Coat of Arms, with a Cock. The Cannon, in a landscape; an etching, 1518. The Triumphal Car of Maximilian I., in eight sheets, on wood. Six cuts of ornaments for tapestry and embroidery, also on wood. It has been decided by most of the best judges that he probably did not execute the woodcuts himself, but that they were done from his designs. The same decision applies to many of the other German masters, whose names appear on wooden cuts.

In the South Kensington collection are, besides others, impressions of the coats of arms, and a fair collection of his woodcuts. There should be a few more examples of this great master, if possible.

In the British Museum there is a very fine collection of his works.

EDELINCK, Gérard, born at Antwerp 1640; died at Paris 1707. This admirable artist received his first instruction from Cornelius Galle. He was invited by Colbert to Paris in 1665, where he was taken into the service of Louis XIV., who gave him a salary and apartments in the Gobelins. He was received into the academy, and soon afterwards knighted by the king. He worked entirely with the graver, and his execution is at the same time both bold and masterly. His style is delicate and picturesque, and never shows carelessness in details. He engraved 86 medals (80 heads and six reverses), and also several vignettes, titles, theses, &c.

There are impressions of several of his portraits at South Kensington.
The British Museum has a fair collection of his works.

ENGELBRECHT, Christian and Martin, flourished about 1721, at Augsburg. These were two engravers and printsellers, of whom the former, conjointly with J. A. Peefel, engraved some ornamental works for goldsmiths, after *A. Morrison;* and some views for the History of Architecture, published in 1721 by J. Hernhard. Martin Engelbrecht executed some plates after *Rugendas* and other masters, and some prints for Ovid's Metamorphoses.

FALDA, Giovanni Battista, born at Valdugia, circa 1640. It is not known by whom this artist was instructed, but his style resembles that of Israel Silvestre. We have by him several designs and engravings of the select views of the churches and other public places at Rome, embellished with figures, which are neatly drawn. His plates are tastefully etched. In 1676 he engraved a view of the city of Rome, in 12 sheets. There are also by him,—Two views in Rome; the Basilica of St. Peter's, and the fountain of St. Peter's. A large plate of St. Peter's with the buildings round it, 1662. A view of the interior of St. Peter's, on the occasion of the beatification of St. Francis de Sales. A view of the castle of St. Angelo, with the statues on the bridge.

The collection at South Kensington has specimens of his architecture and antiquities in books.

FIALETTI, Odoardo, born at Bologna 1573; died at Venice 1638. This painter was a pupil of Cremonini at Bologna, and afterwards of Tintoretto at Venice. He has etched a great number of prints from his own designs and after other masters. They are executed in a masterly style, and his design is both graceful and correct. Among them we find a set of six friezes of trophies, *after Polidoro da Caravaggio;* 10 grotesques, *after Zancarli;*

13 similar (lengthwise), *after Zancarli;* 74 of costumes of all religious orders; and others.

In the library at South Kensington there is a copy of his book of religious costumes, Paris. Sm. 4to., 1658, "Briefve histoire de l'Institution des Ordres "Religieux."
There is a fine collection of his works in the British Museum.

FINIGUERRA, Maso, born circa 1415; date of death not known. To this artist, a Florentine goldsmith and enameller, we owe, as it is believed on the best authority, the origin of the modern art of engraving, or rather of taking impressions of engraved plates. Nothing is certainly known of the manner in which the discovery was made, but it is conjectured with the greatest appearance of probability that it was found out mainly by accident. Finiguerra, like most of his fellow-artists of that time, was in the habit of engraving silver plates, the work on which was afterwards filled in with a black composition called *niello*, which became hard, and served both to preserve the fine lines and tracery on the plate, which was then immediately polished, and also to show the contrast of the engraving with the rest of the bright surface. By some fortunate chance, an impression was taken by Finiguerra from one of these plates before the application of the *niello*, and this led to the use of paper and printers' ink, and the manufacture of plates intended for the production of prints. We have several impressions from undoubted works of Finiguerra, and as the plates still exist in most cases, with records of their authenticity, they are capable of verification. They are generally full of ornamental detail, such as might be expected from the hand of the great Florentine goldsmith, but the figures are drawn, and the heads and faces touched, with the utmost beauty of delicacy and refinement.

In the British Museum is a sulphur impression of his celebrated Pax, and other valuable and beautiful specimens. In the South Kensington are only facsimiles of some of these rare works.

FOURDRINIÈRE, Pierre, flourished circa 1730. He resided chiefly in London, and engraved several plates for the embellishment of books, plays, and pamphlets. He also executed some large plates of architectural views, which are his best performances, some of which were for a large folio volume of the *Villas of the Antients*, published by Robert Castel in 1728. He also engraved some of the plans and elevations of Houghton Hall.

FOUTIN, J., flourished circa 1619. This engraver was probably a goldsmith, as the only works we know by him are some plates of ornamental foliage, with grotesque heads, figures, &c. They are signed *J. Foutin, à Chasteaudun*, 1619.

Some ornaments by this artist are preserved at South Kensington.

FRISIUS, Hans Vredeman, born at Leuwarde, in Friesland, 1527. This old Dutch engraver was also an eminent architect, and was employed to erect the triumphal arch for the entry of Charles V. into Antwerp. We have by him a book of monuments, entitled *Cœnotaphiorum, tumulorum et mortuorum*

Monumentorum, published at Antwerp in 1563 by Jerome Cock. The plates are etched and finished with the graver with considerable intelligence.

In the South Kensington collection are some specimens of his funeral monuments and trophies of arms, &c.

FROSNE, Jean, born at Paris, circa 1630. This artist was principally employed in engraving portraits, but he also engraved part of the large ornamental plates for the collection of Views, &c. by S. de Beaulieu.

GALESTRUZZI, Giovanni Battista, born at Florence 1618. This painter, whose pictures are little known, was the pupil of Furini, and went afterwards to Rome. He was rather celebrated as an engraver, being the friend of Stefano della Bella, whose style he imitated, and some of whose plates he is thought to have completed after his death. He etched a great number of plates, among which the following are some of the most important: — Several sets of friezes and bas-reliefs after *P. da Caravaggio*. A set of antique gems, with explanations by Leonardo Agostino, published at Rome in 1657 and 1659. Six plates of the mausoleum of Cardinal de Mazarin, from the designs of the *Abbé Elpidius Benedictus*, 1661.

In the South Kensington collection are some vases, &c., by him, after *Caravaggio*. He is fairly represented in the British Museum.

GALIMARD, Claude, born at Troyes (Champagne) in 1729. This engraver passed some time at Rome, and on his return to Paris became a member of the Academy. He engraved, beside other and larger works, a number of ornaments for books, of which 14 frontispieces and vignettes, after the younger Cochin, are particularly described by M. de Heineken.

GALLE, Philip, born at Haerlem in 1537. He was the first of a family of engravers who became very conspicuous in the art. He established himself at Antwerp. He possessed great talent; his design was not incorrect, and his command of the graver shows considerable facility; but his plates, like those of many of his contemporaries, are wanting in harmony. He engraved the Seven Wonders of the World, and the Ruins of Vespasian's Amphitheatre at Rome; eight plates, *after Martin Hemskerk*.

This artist is fairly represented in the British Museum. His " Roman Emperors," and some plates of ornaments, are in the South Kensington collection.

GARNIER, Noel, flourished circa 1560 in France. This artist engraved some wooden cuts, and is also said to have been one of the first who made use of the graver in his country. His plates are very rudely executed, and seem like the productions of a goldsmith. He engraved a set of grotesque ornaments, and 48 figures representing the arts, sciences, trades, &c.

GENTSCH, Andreas, flourished at Augsburg, circa 1616. This old German engraver executed some plates of grotesque ornaments, some of which are dated 1616. He usually marked his works with the same monogram as that of Aldegrever, but it is not difficult to distinguish them by the difference of date, and the inferiority of the plates by Gentsch.

GHEYN, or GHEIN, Jacob, the Elder, born at Antwerp 1565; died 1615. This engraver was taught drawing by his father, who was a glass-painter; and learnt engraving under Goltzius, whose style he imitated. His plates evince a great command of the graver; his style is bold and free, and his design is correct and not without taste. He executed a great number of plates, among which the following are some of the most interesting for our present purpose:—A set of 10 plates, called the Masks; *J. de Ghein, inv. et fec.* Twelve plates of Soldiers of the Guards of Rudolph II. These last are very fine, and important in respect of costume and accessories.

There are one or two pieces by this artist at South Kensington. In the British Museum is a fair collection of his works.

GIFFART, Pierre, born at Paris 1648. He engraved a considerable number of portraits and book-ornaments, which are neatly executed with the graver, but without much taste, though his merit was sufficient to obtain for him the appointment of engraver to the king. We have by him, among others, a set of medals, from the French King's cabinet; a set of ornaments, after *Berain.*

In the British Museum are some of his portraits only.

GIORGIO, Giovanni, flourished at Padua, circa 1650. This engraver worked principally for the booksellers. He engraved the plates for a collection of antique lamps, published in 1658, entitled *De Lucernis antiquorum reconditis, Patavii*, 1653. He also engraved a frontispiece with figures to a book on Anatomy by J. Vesling, dated 1647, signed *Joan Georgius Patavii.*

GOAR, Van, —, flourished in Germany, circa 1516. This artist worked in wood and was principally employed by the booksellers. His cuts are chiefly frontispieces and book ornaments, but they are executed with so much spirit, and in so masterly a style, that his prints are much esteemed. He usually marked his prints with a cipher.

GOUJON, O. *See* RAEFFE.

GUERIN, Christophe, born at Strasburg 1758. This designer and engraver was keeper of the Strasburg Museum, and was living in 1831. He engraved several plates of antique gems, which are executed with the graver in a neat and finished style.

GUERNIER, René, flourished in France in the seventeentn century. According to Florent le Comte, he excelled in engraving ornaments and grotesque figures.

HALBECK, Hans, flourished circa 1618.   This engraver was a native of Copenhagen, and executed a variety of prints, entirely with the graver, in a stiff and formal style.   Among other plates he engraved a set of grotesque ornaments, dated 1618, and a large plate of the heads of the Emperors from Julius Cæsar to Ferdinand II.

HECKINS, Abraham, flourished circa 1634.   This artist is supposed by Strutt to have been a goldsmith.   He engraved a set of ornaments for goldsmiths and jewellers, executed in a neat style.   They are signed, *Abraham Heckins, inv. et Cælator,* 1634.

The South Kensington collection has a few plates of ornament by this engraver.

HEUMAN, Georg Daniel, flourished circa 1724.   This engraver was a German and resided at Nuremberg.   He engraved a set of architectural views of the churches and other public buildings at Vienna, published by John Andrew Peeffel, at Augsburg, in 1724.   They are neatly executed.

HIRSCHVOGEL, Augustin, born at Nuremberg, circa 1506. A german painter in enamel, and engraver.   He was the son of a glass-painter, who taught him the principles of design.   We have several etchings by him, which possess considerable merit.   He usually marked his plates with the date and a cipher.   Among his principal prints are,—A vase, with goldsmith's ornaments, 1543 ; and, A sword, the handle ornamented with eagles' heads, and the scabbard with goldsmith's ornaments.

This artist is fairly represented in the British Museum.

HOEFNAGEL, Georg, born at Antwerp 1546 ; died 1600. He was the son of a diamond merchant, but was allowed by his father to devote himself to art.   He travelled in Italy, where he made drawings of the principal monuments, and on his return to Flanders published a volume of plates, engraved from the designs he had made on his journey.   He then applied himself to painting with some success.   He engraved views and maps for books.   He executed a map or plan of Bristol.   In conjunction with F. Hogenberg and S. Novellani, he engraved the plates for *Braun's Civitates Orbis Terrarum,* published at Cologne in 1572 ; and some of the plates for the *Theatrum Orbis Terrarum,* by Abraham Ortelius.

There is a fair collection of his works in the British Museum.

HOLLAR, Wenceslaus, born at Prague 1607; died 1677. This celebrated engraver was of an ancient family, and was well educated by his parents. He was intended for the law, but devoted himself to engraving at Frankfort, under the tuition of Matthieu Merian. He travelled through Germany, designing and engraving views of the cities through which he passed, which were greatly admired. The Earl of Arundel, then ambassador at the court of Ferdinand II. in 1636, retained him in his employment, and brought him to England on his return home. His prints amount in number to about 2,400. He died in penury and misery. His works are distinguished by surprising lightness and spirit; they are etched with a point which is free, playful, and at the same time firm and finished. Some of his views of abbeys, churches, and ruins, are admirably executed; and no less so his furs, shells, muffs, fans, gloves, tippets, &c. He etched a set of 28 plates, entitled *Ornatus Muliebris Anglicanus*, representing the dresses of English women of all ranks; very fine. Also several plates of the different dresses of the nations of Europe, very fine and scarce. A magnificent chalice, adorned with figures, from a drawing by *Andrea Mantegna*, 1640. And many other beautiful ornamental plates.

There are a good many examples of this able artist in the South Kensington collection; and there is a very fine collection of his works in the British Museum.

HOPFER, David, born at Nuremberg, circa 1510. We have by this artist a great variety of spirited etchings. He handled the point with great freedom and spirit, and his plates are executed in a very pleasing style. He chiefly excelled in ornamental buildings and decorations. He was the eldest of three brothers, who worked in the same manner, but he was also the ablest and most industrious of the three. They marked their plates with a hopblossom (*Hopfer*) between the initials of their names. Among the principal works of this engraver we may notice,—The representation of an altar, MDXXVII. A large altar, with the Virgin, Christ, and S. John. Grotesque figures dancing, of various sizes. The Fountains, ornamented with figures. Military ornaments, with grotesque figures. (Bartsch describes 45 ornamental prints by him.)

There are some fair specimens of this artist at South Kensington. A very fine collection of his works is in the British Museum.

HOPFER, Hieronymus, born circa 1515, at Nuremberg; the younger brother of David. His plates are etched in the style of his elder brother, but are not equal to them. Among them we find (described by Bartsch) 10 plates of vases, and other decorative designs.

There are some specimens of this artist at South Kensington; and a very fine collection in the British Museum.

HOPFER, Lambert, born circa 1515, at Nuremberg. This was the youngest brother of David Hopfer. Among other ornamental pieces he engraved,—An arabesque ornament, with four candelabra; this is esteemed his best print. An altar in a church, with the marriage of S. Catherine. (Bartsch describes 12 ornamental prints by this engraver.)

L H

There are fair examples of his work in the South Kensington collection; and a very fine collection in the British Museum.

HUQUIER. *See* MEYSSONIER.

JACQUART, Antoine de, a native of France, seventeenth century. This engraver has left us some small vignettes, with figures and grotesque ornaments which he usually marked with the letters A. D. I. F. He is mentioned by Florent le Comte.

There are some good specimens of his ornament at South Kensington. In the British Museum there is a very fine collection of his prints.

JACQUEMART, Jules Ferdinand, born at Paris, Sept. 1837. An eminent living artist, by whom we have a variety of exquisite etchings of ornamental subjects, such as crystals, china, metal-work, and all kinds of objects of art. They are executed with a most delicate point, and with great freedom they combine correct-ness of design and faithful expression of texture. He has illus-trated the " Gemmes et joyaux de la couronne conservés au Musée " du Louvre, Par M. H. Barbet de Jouy "; " L'histoire de la " Porcelaine, par A. Jacquemart et E. Le Blant "; &c., &c.

There is a fine collection of his works in the British Museum.

JAMITZER, or JAMNITZER, Christoph, born at Nurem-berg, circa 1560. This artist published a set of grotesque subjects in 1600, etched with lightness and spirit. There are prints also by him with the date 1610.

There are a few of his etchings in the South Kensington collection.

JANSSENS, H., a Flemish engraver, by whom we have some plates of ornaments for goldsmiths and jewellers, enriched with figures and other embellish-ments, and executed in a neat and delicate style. Some of his prints are from his own designs, and others after *H. Tangers* and other masters.

The South Kensington collection possesses some odd plates of ornaments by this artist.

JOLLAT, flourished circa 1510 in France. This artist, mentioned by Papillon, executed the cuts of ornamental borders, figures, &c. for a missal in octavo, published at Paris in 1490; as well as those for an anatomical work by Carolus Stephano, M.D., which bear dates between 1530 and 1532. Though not well drawn, they are very neatly cut.

JUVARRA, Filippo, flourished at Rome, circa 1722. This Italian architect designed and etched a set of ornamental shields, published at Rome 1722 ; they are executed in a bold and free manner, and possess great merit.   He signs them *Car. D. Filippo Juvarra, Architetto e Academico di S. Luca.*

There is a set of the above-described shields in the South Kensington collection.

KERVER, Jacob, flourished at Frankfort, circa 1540. This was a wood engraver, to whom are attributed a set of wooden cuts of grotesque figures, standard bearers, &c., in the old German taste, published at Frankfort in 1540, as well as other prints.   He usually marked his prints with a cipher, to which he sometimes added a knife with a snail on the top of it.   (A similar mark was used by Jacob Kobel.)

KERVER, Thielman, flourished early in the 16th century. There are many devotional books, missals, &c., with woodcuts to the borders, printed at that period, which bear the name of this artist on the title.   Zani mentions him as a designer and engraver ; he was probably a bookseller also.

KESSEL, Theodor, born at Antwerp, circa 1620.   A Flemish engraver, who engraved several plates, many of which are etched, and others assisted with the graver, in a free and spirited manner.   He etched the plates for a volume of vases and ornamental compartments, in eight parts, from the designs of *Adam de Viane*, published at Utrecht.   Most of them are marked with the initials of the designer, and with his own cipher.   He also engraved other subjects.

KIP, Jan, born at Amsterdam, circa 1655 ; died in Westminster 1722.   This artist came to England not long after the Revolution.   He engraved very many plates of views of the palaces and seats in this country, chiefly after the designs of Leonard Knyff ; also a large view of Greenwich Hospital, and the exterior and interior of the Danish Church, built by Cibber.

A set of arches by this engraver is in the South Kensington collection.   He is fairly represented in the British Museum.

KRAUS, Johann Ulrich, born at Augsburg in 1645 ; died 1719.   This engraver, who imitated the style of Le Clerc, copied several of the prints by Dürer and Lucas van Leyden. He also engraved perspective views, and other subjects for the booksellers.   We find by him 13 plates of the most interesting views in Nuremberg, and a view of S. Peter's at Rome, a fine print.

There is a fair collection of his works in the British Museum.

KÜSELL, Matthias, born at Augsburg 1621; died 1682. This artist has engraved several plates, both with the point and the graver, in a style that does him great credit.   Among others are a set of 42 etchings of the scenes and decorations of an opera, *after L. Burnacini,* 1668.

Küsell, Melchior, born 1622, at Augsburg; died 1683. The younger brother of the last-named artist. We have a great number of plates engraved by him in a highly finished and very agreeable style, among which we may mention the scenes and decorations for the opera *Paride ed Elena* of Glück (2nd edition).

Langley, Thomas Batty, flourished in the early part of 18th century, died 1751. This artist was much admired in his day. He was a native of England, and published works on Gothic architecture, and ornaments pertaining thereto, with plates designed and engraved by himself; and other similar works, interesting to the antiquary.

Langlois, Jean, born at Paris 1649; died circa 1712. After learning the rudiments of design in his native city, this engraver went to Rome, where he was received as a member of the French Academy. He engraved several plates from the antique statues, and some architectural subjects from *Andrea Palladio*, as well as other prints.

Laulne, or Laune, Etienne. *See* Delaune.

Lauri, Giacomo, born at Rome circa 1570. This artist published in 1612 a set of 166 prints entitled *Antiquæ Urbis Splendor, &c.*, consisting of views of the ancient buildings of Rome. They are executed with the graver, but are not very good.

Le Keux, John, born at London 1783; died 1846. This eminent architectural engraver was a pupil of Basire, from whom he caught a taste for Gothic architecture. He formed for himself an admirable style, which combined truth and correctness with freedom and spirit. His talent was peculiar and almost unprecedented in his own line, and he has made the fame of many noble buildings which were before neglected or unknown. His works have been instrumental in widely diffusing a taste for the Gothic style. They may be recorded by merely enumerating nearly all the best publications illustrative of Gothic architecture which appeared during his time: Britton's Architectural Antiquities, Cathedrals, &c.; the elder Pugin's Antiquities of Normandy, Gothic Specimens, and Gothic Examples; Neale's Westminster Abbey (in which the interior of Henry VII.'s chapel is a wonderful performance). The plates in the first volume of Neale's " Churches " are also by him; as are the " Memorials of Oxford " and the similar work on Cambridge, both chiefly after drawings by Mackenzie, and two most charming works of their kind.

There are many of his works, architectural and various, distributed among books in the South Kensington Art Library, which are named above.

Leyden, Lucas Jacobsz, called Lucas van, born at Leyden 1494; died 1533. Among the artists of his country, none have been more remarkable than Lucas van Leyden. At the early age of nine years, he devoted himself to unremitting study and laborious practice of Art; and he may be said never to have relaxed the habit of continuous application until the day of his death. Taught at first by his father, he afterwards studied under Cornelius Engelbrechtsen, when he astonished the artists of the day by his picture of St. Hubert, painted when he was 12 years old. His prints, some of which (and not the least important) were engraved at the age of 14 and 16, are delicately and beautifully  executed, and we must admire in them the most perfect composition, a thorough knowledge of perspective, and excellent rendering of distance. There is in them something very like aerial perspective in a painting. Among these admirable prints,—many of which are full of ornamental and decorative detail, such as the border of foliage round the nine circular plates of the Passion,— we have also 11 plates representing panels and circles of ornament, charged with sphinxes, amorini, sirens, tritons, &c., amid tracery of foliage and arabesques.

There are a few specimens of this great master in the South Kensington collection, including the set of the Passion, and one or two more, as well as two or three plates of ornaments. In the British Museum is a very fine collection of his works.

LOGGAN, David, born at Dantzig 1630. He is said to have been taught by Simon Pass, and afterwards by Hondius. He was employed in England in engraving views of the public buildings of Oxford, which were published collectively in folio in 1675, under the title of *Oxonia Illustrata*, 40 plates. He engraved and published a similar vol. for Cambridge in 1688, 30 plates. He also executed a set of 11, entitled *Habitus Academicorum Oxoniæ à Doctore ad servientem*. There are also a great number of portraits by him.

He is admirably represented in the British Museum.

LOWRY, Wilson, born circa 1770 ; died 1824. This very eminent English engraver was an apprentice to John Browne the landscape engraver. He engraved most of the plates for Rees's Cyclopædia, Crabbe's Technological Dictionary, the Philosophical Magazine, and other works of a like kind. His mathematical knowledge, his deep researches in the laws of mechanics, his extensive acquaintance with physics, joined to a very great correctness of eye and hand, highly qualified him for such works. Some of the finest specimens of his abilities as an architectural engraver, are to be found in the plates of Murphy's Batalha, Nicholson's Architecture, the print of the House of Commons at Dublin, and Gandon's designs.

In the British Museum is a fine collection of his works.

LUCAS, of LEYDEN. *See* LEYDEN.

LUTMA, Jacob, flourished at Amsterdam, circa 1670. He etched and finished with the graver a set of plates of ornamental shields and foliage ; they are executed in a neat style, from the designs of Jan Lutma, an older artist of the same family.

He might with advantage be represented by a few examples at South Kensington.

LUYKEN, Jan, born at Amsterdam 1649; died 1712.
A scholar of Martin Zaagmoelen, who began as a painter, but
afterwards devoted himself to engraving. From his facility of
invention and execution he gained the name of the Callot of
Holland. His prints possess considerable merit, though inferior
to the works of the great artist after whom he was called. He
executed a great variety of emblematical subjects, public ceremonies,
book ornaments, &c.

He is fairly represented in the British Museum.

MANASAR, Daniel, flourished at Augsburg, circa 1626.
This artist engraved chiefly plates of architecture, plans of buildings, &c., which are executed entirely with the graver, in a neat
but stiff style. Conjointly with W. Kilian, he engraved the plates
for a work entitled *Basilicæ S. S. Udalrici et Afræ Augustæ
Vindelicorum Historiæ*, published at Augsburg, 1626. His prints
are generally marked D. M. F.

MANTEGNA, Andrea, born near Padua 1431; died 1506.
This distinguished painter and engraver was the son of a herds-
man, and his first occupation was watching cattle. Having shown
a taste for art, he was taken into the school of Fr. Squarcione,
where his progress was so wonderful that his instructor adopted
him as his son. He married the daughter of Jacopo Bellini.
Among his principal pictures was the set of the Triumph of Julius
Cæsar, painted for the Palazzo di S. Sebastiano at Mantua, for

which he was knighted by the Marchese *di*
Mantua; and these are also engraved by
himself in nine plates, and are replete with
admirable and useful ornamental details,
and models for the student of decorative art.
There are other prints by this great master, among which is the
magnificent Chalice which was copied by Hollar.

In the South Kensington collection is a complete set of the Triumph of
J. Cæsar (with the pilasters); and a very fine set of his works in the British
Museum.

MARCHANT, Pierre, flourished circa 1623.
The name of this engraver is affixed to a book of
goldsmith's ornaments, executed with the graver
in a neat but free manner. It is signed *Petrus
Marchant, fecit*, 1623.

MAROT, Jean, born at Paris 1620. We have by this
artist, who was an architect, 25 plates of plans and elevations of
the most remarkable edifices in Paris and the vicinity. He
engraved also 21 plates of views of the Château de Richelieu, and
three plates of plans and elevations of the Louvre, three similar
of the Château de Vincennes, and two of the Château de Madrid.

In the South Kensington collection is his " Recueil des Plans," &c., 4to.,
Paris, 1670, and other examples.

MAROT, Daniel, born at Paris 1650. He was the son of
the last-named artist, and distinguished himself as an architect

and an engraver. He engraved several plates in the style of his father, which were published at Paris with some by Jean Marot; also a set of architectural plates, which were published at Amsterdam 1712; and the statues and vases in the Palace at Loo. He engraved many others.

There are several pieces of ornament by this artist in the South Kensington collection.

MECHELN, or MECKENEN, Israel von, father and son, flourished circa 1460, or 1480. The father is said to have been born at Bocholt in Munster, in Westphalia, in 1424; the son died in 1523. They were painters as well as engravers. Their style is precise and hard, and it is difficult to distinguish that of the father from the work of the son. Their prints are rather numerous, and among them we find a good many of an ornamental character. We may mention a variety of goldsmith's ornaments, a cup, richly decorated, which has also been engraved by Martin Schön, and coats of arms. The real name of these masters is not known. Their influence on contemporary art was very great.

In the British Museum is a very fine collection of their works. They are well represented at South Kensington by several important prints of ornament.

MEISSONIER, or MEYSSONIER, Justus Aurelius, born at Turin 1695. This artist was a painter, a sculptor, an architect, a goldsmith, and an engraver. He chiefly resided at Paris, where he was made goldsmith to the King by patent, and was appointed first designer in his cabinet. He etched some plates of ornaments, &c., and has left a great number of architectural drawings and designs for goldsmiths, several of which were afterwards engraved by Huquier.

In the Art Library, South Kensington, there is a copy of his "Livre d'ornemens, &c.," 7 plates, Paris, n.d.

MIGNOT, Daniel, flourished circa 1593. This French artist was probably a goldsmith, as we find his mark on prints of ornaments used in that trade. There are also architectural ornaments by his hand.

Several ornamental pieces by this artist are in the South Kensington collection.

MODENA, Niccoletto da, born at Modena, circa 1460. This early artist was a painter of architecture and perspective, but better known as an engraver, being one of the very first who practised that art in Lombardy. He has left us a variety of prints, numbering about 86, many of which contain a great deal of valuable ornamental detail, and

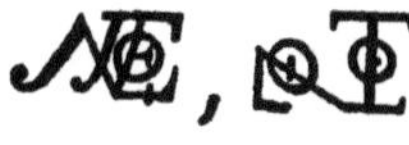

among which there are six plates of ornamental designs for goldsmiths or other artizans.   One of his plates is in the *niello* style.

A fine collection of his works is in the British Museum.

MONCORNET, Balthazar, born at Rouen 1630 ; died 1670.
He lived chiefly at Paris, where he followed the business of
a printseller.   He engraved an almost incredible number of
portraits, besides other plates ; among which we may mention
the Triumph of Constantine, *after Rubens ;* a set of ornaments
for goldsmiths ; and "Le branle des Modes depuis François I.
jusqu'en 1665."

There are some pieces of ornament by him at South Kensington.

MOREAU, P., flourished circa 1750.   This was a French
architect, who designed with great taste, and etched some plates
of architectural subjects from his own compositions.

There is a fair collection of these prints in the British Museum.
At South Kensington there is a drawing of a ceiling by him, but none of
his prints.

MORGHEN, Philip, born at Naples, circa 1730.   This
artist was probably the brother of John Elias Morghen, by whom
he was instructed in engraving, and in conjunction with whom he
executed part of the plates for the Antiquities of Herculaneum,
published at Naples, 1757.   We have also by him 31 Views and
Ruins in the environs of Naples.

NEALE, John Preston, born 1770 ; died 1848.   A very
eminent English architectural designer and engraver.   In 1818
he published the first portion of the "History and Antiquities of
" Westminster Abbey," and in 1823 the second part, forming
together two vols. royal quarto, containing 61 beautiful engravings
by his hand.   At the same time with the first of these volumes
he published six other vols. royal quarto of " The Seats of Noble-
" men and Gentlemen of England, Wales, Scotland, and Ireland ;"
and in 1829 a second series of five vols., containing in the whole
737 plates.   He was indefatigable, and produced in conjunction
with Le Keux another work containing 98 plates in the years
1824 and 1825, entitled "Views of the most interesting Collegiate
" and Parochial Churches, &c."   He also painted architectural
subjects in oil, but abandoned that art for engraving, which was
more congenial to him.   He was one of the most eminent of the
pictorial recorders of our national architecture.

In the Art Library, South Kensington, are six views of Blenheim Palace,
1823, by this artist.

NICOLET, Benedict Alphonse, born at St. Imer, Basle,
1740; died 1807.   This artist went to Paris when young.   He
engraved several of the plates which embellished the *Voyage
Pittoresque du Royaume de Naples*, by the Abbé de St. Non.
He also executed a view of the interior of the church of S.
Januarius at Naples, *after Duprés.*

NOLLI, Giovanni Battista, flourished circa 1755.   This
artist engraved several plates of plans and views of buildings.

He was the father of Carlo Nolli, who was employed by the King of the two Sicilies in executing the plates of the antiquities discovered at Herculaneum.

NORDEN, John, born in Wiltshire, circa 1546. This English artist was an eminent engraver of topographical subjects. He lived at Hendon, and was surveyor of the king's lands in 1614. His principal work was his *Speculum Britanniæ*, an historical and chorographical description of Middlesex and Hertfordshire, with a frontispiece and maps. He also engraved a view of London in 1603, with a representation of the lord mayor's show, with a variety of habits.

In the Art Library, South Kensington, there is a copy of his " Surveyor's Dialogue," London, 1607.

ORAZZI, Niccolo, flourished circa 1760. He was employed in executing some of the plates for the *Antiquities of Herculaneum*, published by the authority of the King of the two Sicilies.

PADTBRUGGE, H. L., born at Stockholm, and flourished circa 1700. He engraved the greater part of the plates for a work called *Suecia Antiqua et Hodierna*, in three vols. folio, vol. i. published in 1693, and the last vol. in 1714. It contains about 350 plates of bird's eye views and maps, executed in a free and spirited style.

PAPILLON, Jean, the younger, born at St. Quintin 1661; died 1723. After receiving some instruction from his father he was sent to Paris, where he was placed under the tuition of Noel Cochin. He turned his attention to engraving on wood, and his cuts possess considerable merit. This artist is said to have been the inventor of printing papers in imitation of tapestry, for furnishing walls of rooms, about 1688. He executed a great variety of book ornaments. He was the first who engraved on wood with the point without beginning with the pen.

There is a good collection at South Kensington of ornamental woodcuts, vignettes, &c. by this artist.

PAPILLON, Jean Baptiste Michel, born at Paris 1698; died 1776. This was the son of the preceding artist, and was instructed by his father in the art of engraving on wood, which he practised with great success. He published an interesting history of that art, in two vols., entitled *Traité historique et pratique de la Gravure en bois*. In this work are inserted many beautiful specimens of engraving on wood, some of which are executed with single uncrossed lines, producing a clear and pleasing effect. Several of his cuts represent ornamental foliage, flowers, and shells, which give great proof of his ability.

The historical portion has been superseded by later works, but the cuts are not easily surpassed.

There is a copy of his book (Paris. 1766), in the Art Library, South Kensington.

PARASACCHI, Domenico, flourished at Rome, circa 1630. This artist, in conjunction with Giovanni Maggi, engraved a set of plates of the fountains at Rome, published 1618. This collection, with additions, was afterwards republished at Rome in 1636, entitled *Raccolta delle principale Fontane della Città di Roma, disegnate e intagliate da Domenico Parasacchi.*

In the Art Library, South Kensington, is a copy of his Roman Fountains, Roma, 1637.

PARR, Remigius, born at Rochester 1723. This English artist was an architectural designer and engraver, and was chiefly employed by the booksellers in making book ornaments. In 1737 he published a view of London from Westminster Bridge, and others of a similar kind. He was living in 1750.

PASSE, Crispin de, the Elder, born circa 1560. Very little is known with certainty of the life of this eminent artist. He was instructed by Koornhaert, and his first dated work was executed in 1589. The date of the publication of his " Drawing book," 1643, makes him an octogenarian, and later than that there is no account of him. His prints are very numerous, and distinguished by great spirit and delicacy, especially in subjects of a small size. He executed a great many ornamental and emblematical plates for books, in a neat, clear, and original style.

This artist is fairly represented in the British Museum.

There are one or two ornamental pieces by him in the South Kensington collection, and several works by him in the South Kensington library, one of which contains designs for altars, tombs, chimney-pieces, furniture, &c.

PATTE, Pierre, born at Paris 1723 ; died circa 1780, or later. This artist wrote several works on architecture, and engraved some of the plates for Blondel's *Architecture Française;* also Perspective Views, *after Piranesi,* and other similar prints.

PAUTRE, Jean le, born at Paris 1617 ; died 1682. This eminent artist was, in the early part of his life, placed under a carpenter and builder, from whom he learned to draw plans and ornamental designs, in which he discovered an inventive genius and extraordinary facility. He afterwards turned his attention to engraving, both with the point and the graver, and executed a prodigious number of plates, consisting of architectural decorations, friezes, ceilings, vases, mausoleums, altars, tombs, fountains, chimneys, panels, doors, façades, &c., from which much of the modern *renaissance* art has been drawn. His works amount to nearly 1,500 plates. About 700 of them were published by Mariette, collected in four small fol. vols. in 1659 and following years.

In the British Museum Library there are many of this artist's works.

He is well represented at South Kensington by a collection of architectural and decorative details and vases.

PEACKE, Edward, flourished circa 1640. This was an English engraver who, in conjunction with Robert Peacke, who was probably his brother, executed some plates of friezes and other architectural ornaments published in 1640.

PENCZ, or PENS, Georg, born at Nuremberg, circa 1500; died at Breslau 1550. This artist was first instructed in the school of Dürer, and went afterwards to Italy, where he studied the works of Raphael, and engraved several plates under Marc Antonio Raimondi, whose style he successfully imitated. Among about 130 prints, many of which are very interesting for decorative detail, we find a few of purely ornamental design, consisting of grotesque figures mixed with arabesques and foliage.

There is a fine collection of his works in the British Museum.

The South Kensington collection possesses many specimens, in sets or parts of sets of his small prints.

PERAC, Etienne Du, born at Paris, circa 1540; died 1601. This artist went to Italy when young, and lived some time at Rome, where he made many designs from the vestiges of ancient architecture, and views of Tivoli and Frascati, which he engraved and published at Rome in 1569, 1573, and 1575. The latest date on a print by Du Perac is 1583.

Some of the works of this artist are preserved in the Library, South Kensington.

PEREGRINI DA CESENA, or PELLEGRINO DA CESIO, flourished circa 1500. He was a goldsmith, engraver, and worker in *niello*. Scarcely anything of him is known except his works, of which about 64 have been described. As they are very rare, there may be many unique impressions yet undescribed. Most of these bear traces of the influence of the goldsmith's habit of design; and there are, besides, 11 plates of arabesques, a coat of arms, and designs for three knife handles, all by his hand. He marked many of his plates with his initials or a cipher.

There is one ornamental print by this artist in the South Kensington collection, and many of his works in the British Museum.

PERELLE, Gabriel, born at Paris, circa 1610; died 1680. This artist excelled in drawing and engraving landscapes with ruins and temples. He was assisted in his numerous works by his sons, ADAM and NICHOLAS PERELLE, who after his death engraved a great number of plates of architectural views. They worked both with the point and the graver. The large views of public buildings and gardens in France, Italy, and Spain, were published, with those of Silvestre, in 1680; and there is a smaller set by these artists.

There is a considerable number of his prints in the South Kensington collection, and a fine collection of them also in the British Museum.

PERRY, Francis, flourished circa 1700. He was born at Abingdon, and was a pupil of van der Bank, and afterwards of Richardson; but made little progress as a painter. He then turned to engraving, and worked for some time for the magazines. His best plates, however, are coins and medals, which are executed with neatness and precision.

PFEFFEL, Johann Andreas, born 1674; died 1750. This artist lived at Vienna, and was a printseller and engraver. His works were chiefly confined to architecture and ornamental foliage, executed in a neat style. In conjunction with C. Engelbrecht, he engraved a set of plates of jewellery ornaments, from the designs of A. Morison; and part of the plates for the *History of Architecture*, published at Vienna in 1721 by Johann Henhard Fischers. There were two artists of the name J. A. Pfeffel, father and son; the latter died in 1768, aged 53. Their works are not easily distinguished apart.

The Art Library, South Kensington, contains many prints by these artists, including Bible illustrations, German Emperors, trophies of arms, &c.

PICART, Jean, flourished at Paris circa 1640. He is supposed to have been a pupil of Crispin de Passe, whose designs and manner he not very successfully copied. He was employed chiefly in engraving ornaments for books. He also executed several book plates of monuments, &c.

There is a fine set of his works in the British Museum.
The South Kensington collection possesses also some by him, in the Chalçographie du Louvre.

PICART, Bernard, born at Paris 1663; died at Amsterdam 1733. This artist, instructed in design and engraving by his father, gained the prize at the Academy of Paris at the age of 16. His plates amount to about 1,300, many of which are after his own design. They consist chiefly of book plates, and other ornamental engravings, and are executed with the point and graver. He engraved also many frontispieces to books.

There are some specimens of this artist, Religious Ceremonies, &c., in the South Kensington collection; and a fine collection in the British Museum.

PICQUOT, Thomas, flourished circa 1637. An engraver of goldsmiths' work, designs for embroidery, damasking, and other ornaments. He was perhaps a pupil of Marin le Bourgeois, painter and valet-de-chambre to Henri IV. and Louis XIII., whose portrait he engraved. His other works are ornamental designs, arabesque or moresco, for goldsmiths' and armourers' work, book-decorations, &c. They are not numerous, but are etched with an extremely delicate point, and appear in white on a dark ground, as does the monogram with which they are marked.

PIRANESI, Giovanni Battista, born at Venice 1721; died 1779. There is some uncertainty as to the place of his birth and early residence. All writers concur in esteeming him as one of the best designers and engravers of architectural subjects and ruins, and the most picturesque in his arrangements and combinations, of the artists of his time. He had many imitators, but none rivalled him in excellence. He has been called the *Rembrandt of Architecture.* It would be impossible to detail the names of his numerous works; they fill 20 folio volumes mostly published in his lifetime, but several by his son Francesco at Rome. The latter engraved in the same style, and it is difficult to distinguish their works apart in all cases.

A very fine collection is in the British Museum, and his complete works are to be found in the South Kensington collection.

PIRANESI, Laura, born at Rome 1750. This lady was the daughter of G. B. Piranesi, and has engraved some views of the remarkable buildings in Rome, which are executed with taste and delicacy.

A fine collection of her works is in the British Museum.

PITTONI, Battista, born at Vicenza 1520. This artist engraved landscapes with ruins, fabulous subjects, and arabesques. Some of them bear date from 1561 to 1585. There is a work by him entitled *Imagini favolosi, &c., intagliati in Rami da M. Battista Pittoni. In Venetia presso Fran. Ziletti,* 1585. Of his paintings there is no record.

PORRO, Girolamo, born at Padua circa 1520; died circa 1604. He engraved a great number of vignettes for a book entitled *Impressi degli uomini illustri,* by Camillo Camilli. His last work was a set of wood cuts for the *Funerali degli Antichi,* by Tommaso Porcacchi, published at Venice in 1574.

There is a copy of the book of emblems of C. Camilli, Venetia, 1586, in the South Kensington collection.

POULLEAU, born at Paris in 1749. A modern French artist, who has engraved several plates of ruins and architecture; among which are the following :—Ruins of a Temple, *after de Machy;* a view of the interior of the Church of the Madeleine, at Ville l'Evêque, *after Contau d'Ivry.*

QUAST, Peter, born at the Hague circa 1600. This painter has left us numerous prints, etched after his own designs, some of which are in the style of Callot, though incorrect in drawing. He generally marked his prints with a cipher composed of a P and a Q joined together. Among his prints we may cite,—The Four Seasons, in grotesque figures; 26 plates of beggars, &c., and 12 of grotesques.

A fine collection of his works is in the British Museum, and there is a set of the beggars at South Kensington.

QUEWELLERIE, Guillaume de la, flourished circa 1680. This artist was a Frenchman, and probably a goldsmith as well as an engraver. He executed a set of very small plates, representing ornamental crosses, and other designs for jewellery. They are neatly engraved, with dark backgrounds. On the frontispiece is his name, *Guilhelmies de la Quewellerie, fecit, An. Dni.* 1680. On the other plates are the initials G. D. L. Q.

QUILLART, Pierre Antoine, born at Paris 1711. A scholar of Watteau, and an ornamental painter and engraver. He executed, from his own designs, the plates for a book entitled *The Funeral Pomp of Duke Don Nuno Olivares Pereira*, published at Lisbon 1730.

RADEMACKER, Abraham, born at Amsterdam 1675; died 1735. This artist, as a landscape painter, is said to have reached an eminent rank, without the assistance of any instructor. His first productions were painted in water-colours, and were very highly finished ; he afterwards practised oil-painting with no less success. He was also well versed in architecture, and engraved from his own designs a set of plates of the most interesting views of ancient monuments, &c., in Holland and the Netherlands. Three hundred of these were published in six vols., small 4to., at Amsterdam, in 1727.

In the library, South Kensington, is a copy of his " Les plus agréables vuës " de Rhynland," &c., fol., Amsterdam 1732 ; also his " Miroir des délices," fol., Amsterdam, n.d. ; and other works.

RADI, Benardino, flourished circa 1618. This was an Italian designer and engraver, whose name is affixed to a set of architectural ornaments, monuments, &c., published at Rome in 1618. They are slight etchings, and bear the title *Varie invenzioni per depositi di Bernardino Radi cortonese.*

RAEFUS, or RAEFE, P., born at Paris 1540. This was a wood-engraver whose name, according to Papillon, occurs on one of the prints of a cosmographical work by André Thevat, which contains about 200 cuts excellently engraved, the greater part by Raefe. Some of them may have been designed by the celebrated sculptor, Jean Goujon ; but it is certain that an O. Goujon was employed with Raefe, as the prints by him are marked O. G. Jean Goujon flourished about that time, and engraved on wood the figures respecting Masonry in Jean Martin's translation of Vitruvius, published in 1547, which are very highly praised by Dumesnil. They consist of architraves, friezes, columns, and capitals of the several orders of Grecian architecture. Jean Goujon is supposed to have been one of the victims of the Massacre of St. Bartholomew's Day, August 24th, 1572.

RAIMONDI, Marc Antonio, born at Bologna circa 1487 ; died circa 1540. This artist may be regarded as one of the most

extraordinary engravers that has appeared in the art. The purity
of his outlines, and the correctness of his drawing, establish his
merit as a perfect master of design. He worked at first after the
designs of Francia, and copied many of the prints of Dürer. He
afterwards worked entirely for Raffaelle, until his death ; and then
for Giulio Romano. He is said to have
been assassinated by a Roman nobleman,
for having, contrary to his engagement, en-  
graved Raffaelle's Murder of the Innocents
a second time. He brought up two great
pupils in his art, Agostino Veneziano, and Marco da Ravenna,
whose works approach, but do not equal, his own in excellence.
Among the numerous prints engraved by him and these eminent
men, his pupils, are found,—9 plates of capitals, bases, and en-
tablatures of the three orders of columns ; Doric, Ionic, and
Corinthian. Six architectural subjects, vases, &c. Twelve antique
vases of bronze and marble ; and 30 other ornamental and decorative panels and designs.

Agostino Veneziano is represented at South Kensington by some specimens,
and M. da Ravenna by one print, "the Wolf of the Capitol." Marc Antonio
should be well represented.

In the British Museum print room there is a very fine collection of the
works of Raimondi and his scholars.

RAVENNA, Marco (Dente) da, born at Ravenna 
circa 1496. *See* RAIMONDI.

REM, Matthias, flourished circa 1635. This artist engraved
the plates for *L'Architecture de Furtenbach.* He usually marked
his prints with the initials of his name.

In the Art Library, South Kensington, there are copies of the books which
he illustrated.

REUTLIMANN, Johann Conrad, born circa
1600. This was a German goldsmith, who exe- 
cuted some plates of foliage and other orna-
mental designs, published at Augsburg.

ROOKER, Edward, born at London circa 1712. This designer and engraver possessed an admirable talent for engraving
architectural views, of which he has given an extraordinary
example in his large plate of the section of St. Paul's Cathedral,
from a drawing by Wale. There are by him also six views in
London, *after P. Sandby ;* 12 views in England, *after the same ;*
and others.

In the South Kensington collection there is an impression of the plate of the
section of St. Paul's. There is a fair collection of his works in the British
Museum.

ROYER, Jean le, and Aubin-Olivier, lived circa 1550.
These were two brothers-in-law, and both in the service of
Henri II., the one as a medallist, the other as a printer. Both

were skilful engravers on wood, and jointly executed the necessary figures for the illustration of the " Book of Perspective," by Jean Cousin, printed and published by Jean le Royer in 1560. These geometrical figures are very beautiful, and consist of about 60 illustrations. Jean availed himself of his knowledge of design to embellish the works that he printed, so that the greater part of the fleurettes, vignettes, and ornamental letters, in metal or wood, employed in his editions, are his own work.

RUPPRECHT, Friedrich Carl, born at Oberzenn, near Anspach 1779; died at Bamberg 1831. This was a landscape painter, etcher, engraver on wood, and architect, who is best known by his etchings, which are prized for their spirit and finish. There are by him about 24 of these, which include, among various subjects, views of the chapel of St. Elizabeth at Bamberg, the Altenburg, the Monument of Count Adelbert von Badenberg, the Ruins of the Castle of Badenberg, Bamberg from the North Side, the Church of the Capuchins at Bamberg, and a repetition with some variations, and other fine and important architectural views of Bamberg.

SADELER, Johann, born at Brussels 1550; died at Venice circa 1600. This eminent engraver was the son of an engraver of ornaments on iron and steel, which were afterwards inlaid with gold or silver; and he was himself brought up to the same business. He subsequently applied himself to engraving on copper, and learned to draw the human figure correctly, though with some of the stiff formality of his time. Among his numerous works we have by him a portrait of Martin Luther, in an arabesque border, and other ornamental plates.

He is fairly represented in the British Museum collection.

SALY, Jacques François, born at Valenciennes 1717; died 1776. This artist resided in Denmark for some time. He was a sculptor and also an engraver, and executed 30 plates of vases, and four designs for monuments. They are etched with spirit.

There is a set of the above-named vases in the South Kensington collection.

SCHEINDEL, or SCHEYNDEL, Georg van, flourished circa 1635–1660. This engraver, who lived at Rotterdam, engraved some plates in a neat and agreeable style, resembling that of Callot. Among others we have by him a set of four views of a castle and the environs; 12 plates of European, Turkish, and Greek figures; and 12 of costumes of the countrymen of the several cantons of Holland.

SCHLICHT, Abel, born at Mannheim 1754; died 1826. This was a painter and an architect, and also engraved some plates in aquatinta, which are highly praised by Hüber. Among them we find several architectural views, *after Bibiena, Pannini, and others.*

SCHÖN, or SCHONGAUER, Martin, born circa 1450; died 1488. This great artist was probably a native of Colmar. He is said to have united the business of a goldsmith with that of a painter, and to have thus acquired a great command of the burin before he began engraving on copper. It is thought that nearly all his prints were executed in the last 20 years of his life. Scarcely any artist has exercised so much influence over the art of his country as Schongauer. He corresponded with Perugino; his print of the temptation of St. Anthony is said to have been copied, or perhaps only coloured, by Michel Angelo; and Dürer himself is said to have been so much interested by his works as to have made a journey to see him in 1492. He was unfortunately away from home at the time. There is great uncertainty as to his pictures. His prints are numerous, and many of them most interesting to the student of ornamental decoration. Among these are a set of 12 subjects of ornaments for goldsmiths, a ciborium, an incense cup or censer, and a bishop's crozier.

He is very fairly represented at South Kensington, where there are impressions of his set of circles, the censer, the crozier, and other plates. In the British Museum print room there is a very fine collection of his works.

SCOPPA, Orazio, born at Naples circa 1600. This artist was probably a goldsmith. He executed a set of 15 plates of designs for chalices, croziers, and other ecclesiastical ornaments. They are etched in a spirited style.

SILVESTRE, Israel, born at Nancy 1621; died at Paris 1691. This eminent engraver was the nephew of Israel Henriot, by whom he was probably instructed in design and engraving. He formed his style upon those of Callot, Della Bella, and afterwards Le Clerc. He was patronized by Louis XIV., appointed drawing master to the Dauphin, and was made a member of the Academy. His prints amount to upwards of 1,000. Among them we find 13 views in Rome and the environs; 12 views of gardens and fountains; a view of Paris; a large view of Rome, in four sheets; the Grand Carousal, or Royal Entertainment at Paris in 1662; and many others of the same kind.

There is at South Kensington a very large collection of his etchings; and a fair number in the British Museum.

SOLIS, Virgil, born at Nuremberg 1514; died 1562. This artist was an engraver and etcher on copper; he also designed many woodcuts, but it does not appear that he cut them himself, any more than many of the other artists of the time, whose names are found on woodcuts. He was also a painter and an illuminator. It is probable, from the immense number of his prints and the great varieties of style to be observed between them, that they were not all executed by his own hand. Among them we find a set of vases and ornaments for goldsmiths, dated 1541 ; and other decorative plates.

He is well represented at South Kensington by a good collection of his ornamental pieces ; and there is a fair number of them in the British Museum.

SPECCHI, Alessandro, flourished circa 1665–1710. He engraved a set of plates of views of the palaces and public buildings at Rome, which are executed in a bold and spirited style. They were published in 1699.

There is in the South Kensington library a copy of his " Facciate Illuminate " e Fuochi d' artificio in Roma," &c., &c. Folio. Rom. 1722.

STURT, John, born in London 1658 ; died 1730. This engraver was a pupil of Robert White. His chief excellence lay in executing ornamental letters. His principal work was his book of Common Prayer, published 1717, which was very neatly engraved on silver plates. The top of every page was ornamented with a small vignette.

In the South Kensington library is a copy of Perrault's Architecture, for which Sturt engraved the plates and tailpieces. (See also " Pozzo," Perspective.—*U. Cat. Books on Art.*)

TARAVAL, Louis Gustavus, born at Stockholm 1737. This was an architectural designer and engraver, who has left us several architectural plates. He was sent to Paris by his father, Thomas Raphael Taraval, who was a portrait painter.

THULDEN, Theodor van, born at Bois-le-duc 1607; died 1676. This painter was one of the best of the pupils of Rubens. We have a considerable number of etchings by him, in a clear and determined, though rather slight, style ; among which are a set of eight plates of the triumphal arches designed by *Rubens* for the entry of the Cardinal Infant Ferdinand into Antwerp.

In the South Kensington library there is a work by Abbati (N. dell') " Les " travaux d'Ulysse," illustrated by Van Thulden. There is a fair collection of his works in the British Museum.

TOMS, W. H., flourished circa 1740. This engraver executed several architectural subjects, some book plates, and a few portraits. Among the most important, we find four views of Gibraltar, and eight in Jersey.

TREU, Martin, flourished circa 1540. There is no account of an artist of this name, but there is a monogram composed of an M and a T, to which this name has been given. Among the prints undoubtedly by this artist are several ornamental designs, and designs for sheaths, poniards, &c., some of which are dated 1540.

VACCARO, Francesco, born at Bologna circa 1630 ; died 1687. This was a painter and engraver of architectural and perspective views. He published a treatise on perspective, embellished with plates engraved by himself, from his own designs.

He engraved 12 perspective views of ruins, fountains, and other Italian edifices, inscribed Fr. Vaccaro, fec.

VAUGHAN, Robert, flourished circa 1650. This English artist was chiefly employed in executing portraits and other plates for the booksellers. He engraved a monument for Dugdale's Warwickshire, and some of the maps, and other similar works.

He is fairly represented in the British Museum.

VAUQUER, Jean, flourished in the eighteenth century. This artist was a native of Blois in France, and followed the trade of a goldsmith. He engraved, from his own designs, several plates of flowers and ornamental foliage, which he calls *Livres des Fleurs, propres pour orfevres et graveurs.*

There are a considerable number of ornamental pieces, portions of sets, &c. by this artist in the South Kensington collection.

VEENHUYSEN, J., flourished at Amsterdam circa 1660. This artist engraved a set of views of the public buildings in Amsterdam, which are executed in a slight but neat style. They are embellished with figures, which are designed with tolerable correctness. They were published in Amsterdam in 1686, with Dutch and French descriptions.

VENEZIANO, Agostino de Musis, called; born circa 1490; see RAIMONDI.

VICO, Enea, born at Parma circa 1520; died circa 1570. He is said to have been instructed in design by Giulio Romano. Attracted by the great reputation of Raimondi at Rome, he went thither and became one of his pupils. His prints, notwithstanding some faults, are held in high estimation. They are numerous. Among the most important of them we find a set of 12 vases, from the designs of P. da Caravaggio. A set of 50 plates of the habiliments of different nations, from his own designs, &c., &c.

He is well represented at South Kensington by specimens of trophies, vases, and other subjects. There is a fine collection of his works in the British Museum.

VINSAC, Claude Dominique, born at Toulouse 1749. This artist engraved several portraits, and also designs for goldsmiths, in the dotted manner, which are neatly executed.

VITUS, Domenico, born circa 1536. There is little known of the history of this Italian artist. He is supposed to have been a pupil of Agostino Veneziano, whose style he imitated with some success. He became a monk in the prime of his life. We have by him several prints, among which is a set of small plates representing the Passion of our Saviour, with borders ornamented with birds, beasts, &c.; and a set of plates of antique statues.

WALCH, Jacob, flourished circa 1480. This ancient German artist, whose plates are marked with a W and a cross, was a contemporary of Israel van Mecheln, and his prints have some resemblance to those of that engraver. They are designed in the stiff and formal manner of the time, but some of them are highly interesting for their ornamental character and details. Among these we may cite a gothic ornament for a crozier, the inside of a gothic building, and others of a like nature. There is a very fine collection of his works in the British Museum.

WEIGEL, Hans, flourished circa 1535; died 1590. This was a designer, wood engraver, and printer at Nuremberg, who marked his prints H. W. He is known by his book of costumes, and by ornamental book titles, some of which have his initials.

WET, P. F. This artist, the date of whose working is not known, etched some plates of ornamental foliage for goldsmiths and jewellers. They are executed in a slight style.

WILBORN, Nicolas, flourished 1530–36. We have by this artist about 30 prints, most of which are of ornamental character. One of these, the design for the sheath of a poniard, ornamented with foliage and figures, bears his name in full and the date 1536. The others are similar designs for sheaths, vignettes, or other ornaments.

ZAECH, Bernard, flourished circa 1580. Very little is known of this artist, who was probably a goldsmith as well as an engraver. Besides other prints, we have by him a set of 12 designs for goldsmiths' work, consisting of vases and goblets, marked B. Z., 1581.

ZANCARLI, or GIANCARLI, Poliphilos, flourished circa 1624. This was a designer and engraver of ornament, by whom we have 12 plates of antique foliage for friezes. Many of his designs were also engraved by Odoardo Fialetti.

ZOAN ANDREA, flourished circa 1515. This is an imaginary name, given to an early artist, who engraved a number of plates, which he marked with the letters Z. A. He was probably a goldsmith, and his style resembles very much that of Mantegna, Bramante, and G. A. da Brescia. We have by him, besides other prints, 16 ornamental plates of arabesques, enriched with figures and foliage, some of which are, however, excessively rare.

There is a complete set of his "Pilasters" in the South Kensington collection; and a very fine collection of his works in the British Museum.

LONDON:
Printed by George E. Eyre and William Spottiswoode,
Printers to the Queen's most Excellent Majesty.
For Her Majesty's Stationery Office.
[4593.—250.—12/69.]